PADDY'S POT OF GOLD

❦   ❦   ❦

Dick King-Smith

Illustrations by David Parkins

CROWN PUBLISHERS, INC.
New York

Published by Crown Publishers, Inc., a Random House company,
225 Park Avenue South, New York, New York 10003
Originally published in Great Britain in 1990 by the Penguin Group.
CROWN is a trademark of Crown Publishers, Inc.
Manufactured in the United States of America

Library of Congress Cataloging-in-Publication Data
King-Smith, Dick.
Paddy's pot of gold / Dick King-Smith ; illustrations by David Parkins.
p. cm.
Summary: Brigid enjoys making friends with Paddy the leprechaun and
wonders if he has a pot of gold.
[1. Leprechauns—Fiction.] I. Parkins, David, ill. II. Title.
PZ7.K5893Pad 1992   [Fic]—dc20   91-24586
ISBN 0-517-58136-1 (trade)
0-517-58137-x (lib. bdg.)
10 9 8 7 6 5 4 3 2 1
First U.S. Edition

Contents

CHAPTER 1

In the Carrot Patch

It was early on the rainy morning of her eighth birthday that Brigid first met P.V.W.R.H. O'Reilly.

She knew it was early because it was barely light, and she knew it was raining because she could hear it whispering against her windowpane, the soft Irish rain that gave the Emerald Isle its color.

Brigid dressed and tiptoed downstairs, so as not to wake Mother and Dada. Dada was snoring, she could hear. Did Mother ever snore? Brigid had never heard her. She must ask one day.

The kitchen was full of cats, and she opened the back door for them and looked out. The light was growing now, enough for her to see the squatting white shape of her rabbit in his hutch at the far end of the vegetable garden. He looks hungry, Brigid thought. I'll get him a carrot. Mother won't mind if I pull just one. It's my birthday, after all. I'll try and find an ugly old carrot with a fang root.

She put on her old raincoat and her even older boots and walked across the long grass of the little lawn that Dada was always meaning to cut. The grass was soaking wet, quickly reminding her that she had a hole in one boot.

Then it was, as she neared the carrot patch, that suddenly one of the carrots moved. For a moment Brigid could not believe her eyes. She stood stock still, peering through the falling rain in the rising light, and then—it moved again! What was more, it seemed to be upside down, the orange part above, the green below!

Brigid gave herself a vicious pinch, which hurt, so she knew she was not dreaming, and hurrying closer, found herself looking down at a very small man. The orange part, she could now see, was a flaming shock of hair, but everything else about him was green. Not only his clothes but his face and hands, his fingernails, even, were as green as grass.

He stood beside one of Brigid's boots (he was just the height of it) and, looking up at her,

said in a loud, cheerful voice, "It's a happy birthday I'm wishing you!"

Brigid was speechless. As a very small child
she had half believed in the stories that Dada
used to tell her of the little people, but only half.

It's really just a fairy tale, she had thought. Yet here was one! And how in the wide world could he know that it was her birthday?

At last she found her tongue.

"How did you know?" she said.

"Because you can see me," said the little man. "At last you can see me. There are four things needed before any human can see some-one like me, and at last you have them all. First, of course, you must live in Ireland—"

"I do!"

"And then you must be an only child—"

"I am!"

"And it must be your birthday—"

"It is!"

"And on top of those three, you must have a hole in one boot."

"I have!"

"Well, there you are. Once all those four things go together, then and only then can you see a lep."

"A lep?" said Brigid.

"A leprechaun," said the little man. " 'Tis a long, awkward sort of a word, so we shorten

4

it. And it just so happens that the letters 'l-e-p' stand for something else too."

"What?"

"Little emerald people. You'll have heard of the little people?"

"Oh, yes."

"Well, we leps are different from the rest— brownies, gnomes, elves, and such folk, dull fellows all, and with pointed ears, would you believe?"

That's what Dada always said, thought Brigid. The little people had pointed ears and pointed caps on their heads and long pointed shoes on their feet. But this little man's ears were just like hers only much, much smaller, and he wore nothing on his mop of bright red hair. His face was the face of a very old man, seamed and wrinkled like a walnut, but green, of course. To be sure, he wore an old-fashioned tunic and strange, baggy breeches, but his boots were stout and round-toed. They looked as though they would keep the wet out.

"They do," said the leprechaun, though Brigid had not spoken. "Made of frog skin. Nothing better in this climate. Tanned the leather myself, of course. And that reminds me, you'd better let me mend that boot of yours."

"Could you really?" said Brigid. "How clever!"

"Ah, Brigid, Brigid!" said the leprechaun. "Every lep is a shoemaker, were ye never told?"

"How do you know my name?" said Brigid.

"Why, to be sure," said the leprechaun, "I live here. This is my home, here on your dada's little farm. All of your eight years I've been here, but you never saw me."

"Because I never happened to have a hole in my boot on my birthday before!"

"That's right, Brigid, that's right. And it's forgetting my manners I am. I have not introduced myself. My name is P.V.W.R.H. O'Reilly."

"Goodness!" said Brigid. "What a lot of initials you have. What do they all stand for?"

"Ah, now," said P.V.W.R.H. O'Reilly. "Before I tell you, I'd better explain how I came to choose my names."

"You chose them?" said Brigid.

"Yes," said the leprechaun. "We leps don't suffer like you humans, being given names at birth, names that you may well not like in time to come. We wait twenty years or so before we decide what to call ourselves."

"But didn't your mother and father want to choose the names for you?"

"Leps don't have mothers and fathers. To start with, there's no such thing as a female lep."

"Oh. How d'you get born, then?"

"It's a simple business," said P.V.W.R.H. O'Reilly, "but a bit complicated, if you understand my meaning. You know those little round wooden things, a bit like a nut, that grow on oak trees?"

"Oak apples, you mean?"

"You have it entirely. Well, leps hatch out of oak apples. That's the simple bit. The complicated part—which is why there are not that many of us about—is that this can only happen under certain conditions."

"Like the four things that had to happen before I could see you, you mean?"

7

"You have it entirely. First, it can only happen on the stroke of midnight. Second, the wind must be in the southwest quarter. Third, the moon must be full. And fourth, there must be an owl sitting in the oak tree. He doesn't have to hoot, it's not essential, but he must be there. And all that happened to me in the year that a great battle was fought and a great victory won by an Irish general. Which partly explains my choice of names."

"Please," said Brigid, "tell me what they are."

"I will, indeed I will," said P.V.W.R.H. O'Reilly. "The 'P' is for Patrick, the patron saint of our emerald isle. Isn't it thanks to him that we have no snakes, something for which I'm eternally grateful."

I bet, thought Brigid. Why, a little grass snake would seem like the hugest python to someone your size.

"Now, the 'V' and the 'W,' " the leprechaun went on, "stand for Victorious Wellington. That was the name of the general I was telling you about."

"Oh," said Brigid (who was interested in history at school), "but Wellington won the Battle of Waterloo. And that was . . . oh, I've forgotten the date, but it was ages ago."

"1815. You have it entirely."

"But that makes you . . ."

"One hundred and seventy-four years old."

"Oh," said Brigid.

She could not think of anything else to say, but then, fearing that it would appear that she doubted his word, she said quickly, "What about the 'R' and the 'H'?"

"Right-Handed," said the leprechaun. "Almost every lep in the land is left-handed, you know. Soling a boot, now—he'll hold the upper on the boot last with his right hand and tack the sole on with the hammer held in his left. But me—I do it the other way around. As for O'Reilly, well, a common-enough name it is."

"Among leps?"

"Indeed. And so there you have it, Brigid. Patrick Victorious Wellington Right-Handed O'Reilly, at your service! But you may call me Paddy."

PADDY'S POT OF GOLD

So fascinated had Brigid been by the conversation that she had not noticed that the rain had stopped, that the day was now light, and that at that moment Dada was coming out the back door on his way to milk the cow.

"Oh!" said Brigid. "Hide, Paddy, quickly! Dada's coming!"

"It's needlessly worrying you are," said the leprechaun. "Hasn't your dada three good brothers and two good boots and his birthday not for six whole months? All he will see in the carrot patch is carrots."

And after Brigid's dada had come up and given her a hug and wished her many happy returns of the day, he reached down with one hand and ruffled her mop of dark hair and said, "What a funny girl you are!"

"Why, Dada?"

"Standing in the carrot patch talking to yourself! I saw you. I was watching you from the kitchen window," said Dada, and he walked on toward the cowshed.

Brigid reached down with one hand and ruffled a mop of bright red hair.

"Oh, Paddy!" she said delightedly. "I bet you even know what I'm going to say next!"

"I do, I do. You're going to say 'Find me a carrot for the rabbit, an ugly old carrot with a fang root,' " said P.V.W.R.H. O'Reilly.

CHAPTER 2

In the Rabbit Hutch

Brigid opened her presents (the best one was from Mother and Dada—a beautifully illustrated animal encyclopedia) before breakfast, a breakfast that was a birthday treat in itself. Bacon and eggs and drisheen, the black pudding of County Cork, and then Mother's homemade gooseberry jam on new-baked crusty bread spread thick with butter made from the milk of the cow Fillpail.

While they were eating, Brigid said, "Dada?"

"Yes?"

"D'you remember, when I was small, you used to tell me stories about the little people?"

"Of course I do."

"Do you really believe in them?"

"Of course I do. You can't live in Ireland and not believe in them."

"Including leprechauns?"

"Ah, now, leprechauns," said Mother,

"they're different. They belong to the little people, all right, but they're special."

"The leprechaun," said Dada, "is a shoemaker. Do you know that?"

"I think I do," said Brigid carefully.

"And what's more, he wears very special shoes himself. If ever you should meet one, you'll be in no doubt, because he'll be wearing a pair of high-heeled shoes with big silver buckles on them, buckles as big as the shoes themselves."

"I don't think you can . . ." began Brigid. She had been about to say "be right," but quickly changed it to, "I don't think you can see a leprechaun very easily, though, can you?"

"Only if you're carrying a four-leaf clover," said Dada.

"And I'll tell you another thing," he said. "They're mean, leprechauns are. Stingy. Each one carries a little purse, but there's only one shilling ever in it. That way he can never lend you money. 'Sorry,' he'll say, 'I've only got one shilling. 'Tis all I have in the world.' "

"But that's not true," said Mother, "because

14

every leprechaun has a pot of gold buried some-where."

Brigid chewed and thought about this and swallowed and said, "D'you think if there was a leprechaun living here on this farm, he might show us where his pot of gold is?"

Mother and Dada laughed.

"Wouldn't it be nice!" said Mother. "New carpets, new curtains. I'd buy myself one of those washing machines, too."

"And I'd buy a couple more cows and maybe a little flock of sheep. I'd trade in the old tractor for a new one, too, if there was enough gold in the pot," said Dada. "But no leprechaun would tell you where the pot was."

"He might," Brigid said.

After breakfast Brigid set off for the rabbit hutch. She had arranged with P.V.W.R.H. O'Reilly that they should meet there.

"After all," Paddy had said, "if your dada sees you talking there, he'll think you're talking to old Snowy."

"How do you know my rabbit's name?" Brigid had asked.

15

"Why, because I often talk to him myself. Many a good chitchat we've had, old Snowy and me."

"But he never makes any noise, except a grunt now and then."

"Not to you he doesn't, Brigid," Paddy had said. "What you must understand is that we leps can converse with all the animals."

"And they can see you?"

"Sure, sure, without any conditions."

So Brigid had opened the hutch door and not only put in the ugly old carrot with the fang root but at Paddy's request ("Snowy's saying, 'Come inside, do.' Give us a lift up, there's a dear girl.") had put the leprechaun into the hutch as well.

Now as Brigid walked across the lawn she could smell the sea. Though she could not quite see it from the farm, she sometimes thought in stormy weather that she could hear the crash and pounding of the big Atlantic waves that had run unchecked from the coast of far-off America all the way to Bantry Bay.

In the clear, almost windless air she suddenly saw a little column of blue smoke rising from the rabbit hutch.

Immediately horrified thoughts rushed through her mind.

She should have known . . . You can't trust the little people . . . Some of them are spiteful— play mean tricks—do wicked things . . . That leprechaun whom she had thought so nice had tricked her into allowing him into the rabbit hutch so that he could deliberately set fire to it! He would escape and leave poor Snowy to . . . !

She could see no flames, but still those puffs of smoke kept rising, and she ran, her heart pounding, and reached the hutch and wrenched open the wire door.

There inside was her precious Snowy squatting comfortably, staring placidly out of calm pink eyes, while opposite him P.V.W.R.H. O'Reilly sat upon the rabbit's upturned food dish, one green-clad leg crossed over the other, contentedly smoking a pipe. A short-stemmed pipe it was, and from its bowl the blue smoke rose.

"Paddy!" cried Brigid. "What are you doing?"

Paddy took the short pipe out of his mouth to reply.

"It's me nose warmer," he said, and indeed Brigid could see that the tip of his rather bulbous nose was a little rosy, like a ripening apple.

"You're smoking!" said Brigid. "Don't you know that smoking is bad for you? It can shorten your life."

"One hundred and seventy-four is a goodish score, wouldn't you say?"

"But smoking kills people!"

"People, yes. Leps, no. The point is this, dear girl. It's the nicotine in the tobacco leaves that's the trouble, but we leps don't smoke the tobacco leaf at all."

"What are you smoking, then?"

"Seaweed."

"Seaweed?" said Brigid. "But how do you get that?"

We're a good three miles from the sea, she thought, and goodness knows how long it would take you to walk there and back on those little legs, and how would you carry enough anyway?

"Isn't it your dada that fetches it for me?" said Paddy. "Doesn't he go down to the bay every so often with the old tractor and cart and bring back a great load of seaweed and stack it up in little heaps? Then when it's dry, he digs it into the garden for manure. Now, then, in between the wet and the dry, while the stuff is just nicely moist, I help myself to a wee bit of the best of it, and doesn't it make the grandest smoke?" And he stuck the nose warmer back into his mouth and drew on it.

By now Brigid was feeling guilty that she had so quickly, at the first sight of smoke rising from the hutch, believed the worst of P.V.W.R.H. O'Reilly. How could she have thought he would do such a thing? What a dear little man he was, sitting there smoking his seaweed tobacco, green eyes twinkling, while Snowy—his friend, it was plain—gnawed at his carrot.

She looked at the leprechaun's frog-skin boots. High-heeled shoes with big silver buckles, Dada had said they should be. Was Paddy a real leprechaun? And how about the purse with only one shilling in it?

"Paddy," she said. "Could you lend me some money?"

Paddy took a little green purse out of the little green pocket of his little green tunic and opened it and peered in and took out a coin.

"Sorry," he said, "I've only got one shilling. 'Tis all I have in the world."

Dada was right there, thought Brigid. But what about those boots?

"Dada says," she said, "that leprechauns *always* wear high-heeled shoes with big silver buckles."

Paddy took his nose warmer out of his mouth and cackled with laughter, rocking to and fro on the upturned food dish.

"The funny things that folk believe!" he said. "I'll bet he told you that you could see a lep if you carried a four-leaf clover!"

"He did."

"Well, you could, but only if it was your birthday and you were an Irish only child with a hole in one boot, and then you wouldn't need the old clover anyways."

"But the silver-buckled shoes?" said Brigid.

"I doubt you'd find a single lep wearing them nowadays, not if you were to search the length and breadth of Ireland. Such shoes are very old-fashioned."

"But," said Brigid, "you were born . . . hatched, I mean . . . one hundred and seventy-four years ago. Didn't leps wear them then?"

"A few. But the fashion really started long before that. In 1588, to be exact."

"I know that date!" cried Brigid. "That was when the Spanish Armada was wrecked!"

"All around the coast of Britain, including Ireland," said Paddy. "And some of the ship-wrecked Spanish gentlemen came ashore wearing such shoes, and the leps of those days fancied them and copied them. But nowadays it's all frog-skin boots, though some leps prefer to use the hide of the natterjack toad—it has a nice yellow stripe in it. Tell me, now, Brigid, what else did your folk say about leprechauns?"

Brigid took a deep breath.

"Mother said . . ." she began, and then stopped.

"Well?"

"Mother said . . . that every leprechaun has a pot of gold buried somewhere."

"Did she, now?" said P.V.W.R.H. O'Reilly.

"She did. Is it true, Paddy?"

For a little while the leprechaun puffed at his pipe without answering. Then he said, "It might be."

"Oh!" said Brigid, catching her breath.

"And then again, it might not."

"Oh," said Brigid, letting it out again.

CHAPTER 3

On the Tump

The white rabbit Snowy raised his head from the carrot and gave a grunt.

"Oh, sorry, Snowy, I was forgetting," said Paddy. "There's me and the dear girl blathering on, and I've never given her your message."

"Snowy's got a message for me?" said Brigid.

"Indeed he has. Isn't it lucky that now I can act as interpreter between the two of you?"

"It's wonderful!" said Brigid. "What does he want to say?"

"Something he's been wanting to tell you for a long time. It's been worrying him for years—he's often told me—but of course I couldn't pass the message on until you saw me."

"Oh, dear!" said Brigid. "Doesn't he like the food I give him? Isn't his hutch comfy enough? Is he too cold or too warm? Is he ill? What is it?"

" 'Tis none of those things," said Paddy. "He has a little favor to ask, that's all."

"What is it?"

"Would you mind, he says, getting an old sack or a piece of old blanket, and just dropping it over the front of the hutch at nighttime, over the wire door, as you might draw the curtains in your bedroom?"

"Of course I can. I will. But why? Is he cold? I thought you said he wasn't."

"No. It's the fox."

"The fox?"

"Many a night, Snowy says, the old fox comes out of the wood yonder and sits in front of the hutch, staring. Now, he can't get in— Snowy knows that—but to see him sitting there is not pleasant, Snowy says. The fox stares something terrible, especially in the bright moonlight, and he licks his chops and drools. Snowy can put up with the stink of him, he says, but it would be grand not to have to face that stare. He'd be grateful, he says. It gives him insomnia."

"Of course!" said Brigid. "I'll go and get an old sack this minute."

Later, when Brigid had returned with the sack and folded it on top of the hutch, ready for the night, and had lifted P.V.W.R.H. O'Reilly out and set him on his frog-skin–covered feet, they went, at the leprechaun's suggestion, for a walk.

Brigid of course had to walk very slowly, for Paddy's stride was no more than a few inches, and she did not feel she should offer to carry him like a baby. They were heading, she saw, for the little wood on the side of the hill behind the farm, a hill that gave shelter from the wild west winds that blew so often in that part of the world and left the hilltop trees permanently bent almost double.

"It's wonderful," said Brigid again as they walked, "that you can interpret what Snowy says. Can you do it for other animals?"

"Of course," said Paddy. "Or most of them anyways. I wouldn't expect to have all that grand a conversation with a worm or a beetle—I doubt they'd have that much to say—but I understand most creatures."

"Like our farm animals?"

"Indeed, though of course some of them are not blessed with the highest intelligence. Chickens, now, and ducks—I'd call them birdbrained. But I have a chat with the old cow now and again."

"I've often wondered what animals are feeling," said Brigid. "If only they could speak, I thought. And now they can—through you, Paddy. What does Fillpail say?"

"She's a bit of an old moaner, is Fillpail," said Paddy. "Mostly she complains about her food. 'This hay's not fit for a donkey, let alone a purebred Kerry cow.' . . . That sort of thing. For her the grass is always greener on the other side."

"What about the donkey?"

"Ah, now, it's a pleasure to have a talk with Neddy. A thinker, Neddy is. People suppose that because donkeys are stubborn they must be stupid, but it's not so. A donkey is the brightest of your farm animals, barring one other."

"What's that?"

"Why, a pig, of course. Now, a pig has a grand brain. Many a happy hour have I spent in your dada's pigsties, Brigid, listening to the porkers putting the world to rights. Oh, you can have a really intellectual conversation with a pig!"

By now they were entering the wood, and this reminded Brigid of the fox.

"What about wild animals?" she said. "Can you talk with them?"

"Indeed I can," said Paddy. "I live among them, you see. Always have."

"Here in this wood?"

"Here in this wood."

"Will you show me where you live?"

"I will, I will."

How lovely, thought Brigid as they made their slow way among the trees. He's going to show me his house. I can just imagine it. It will be not much bigger than a doll's house, with a thatched roof, I would think, and twisty chimneys and little diamond-paned windows and maybe dog roses growing around the tiny front door. I won't be able to go inside, of course. I am much too big.

"I won't be able to go inside your house, will I?" she said.

P.V.W.R.H. O'Reilly's lined green face split in a grin, and he gave his cackling laugh.

"You will not, dear girl!" he said, shaking his red locks. "And indeed I haven't a house of my own. I'm a lodger. It suits me better. My landlords are most agreeable folk."

"I don't understand," said Brigid.

"You soon will," replied Paddy. "Look yonder."

Brigid looked and saw that they were approaching a little tump or mound that stood in the middle of the wood. A number of old elder trees, their trunks scored with scratch marks, stood on the tump, and all around its well-trodden sides were a dozen or more large holes.

"Why," cried Brigid, "it's the badgers' set! I've often come here to try to catch sight of them, but I never have."

"Ah, they're shy folk, my landlords are," said Paddy.

"You live *here, in* the badgers' set?"

"I do, I do, dear girl. I have three nice rooms and not a penny of rent to pay, and I have my own private entrance."

They had reached the tump now, and Paddy scrambled up its side and pointed to a large hole beneath the roots of one of the elder trees.

"And here it is," he said.

Brigid knelt and peered into the mouth of the tunnel.

"I wish I could see inside," she said. "Tell me what it's like. Three rooms, you said?"

"Yes, and as snug as can be. Six feet underground is a fine place to be, cool in the summertime, warm in the winter. No frost reaches that deep, and there's no dampness, for the tump is well drained. First, there's my bedroom. And that's another thing—my landlords fetch fresh bedding for themselves every now and then, dry grass, bracken, and such, and they bring enough for me so that I lie comfy. Then there's my workroom—that's where I have my cobbler's tools and my boot last and mend the odd shoe. And then there's my storeroom."

Storeroom! thought Brigid. *Every leprechaun has a pot of gold buried somewhere.* That's where it is!

"What do you keep there?" she asked.

"Oh, this and that."

"Like what?"

"Stocks of food for the winter months mostly. Nuts, berries, roots, fruit, and such. I'm a vegetarian, so I am."

"Nothing else? Don't you keep anything else in your storeroom?"

"Oh, I do and I don't," said the leprechaun.

He held out his little green hand and Brigid bent to take it.

"I'll bid you good-bye for now, Brigid," he said. "I take a little nap at this time of the day. I'm not as young as I was, you see."

"Good-bye, Paddy," said Brigid, and she watched as he went down the hole. In the entrance, which was large, he could stand upright, but then he had to bend a little, she could see, as he went down the tunnel till he turned a corner and was lost to sight.

"What a birthday!" Brigid said. She felt for the hole in the side of her boot, thinking of the four conditions that had allowed her to see P.V.W.R.H. O'Reilly. And as she did so she felt a sudden chill of fear. "It must be your birthday," he had said as one of those conditions, but what if you could only see a leprechaun *on* your actual birthday? What about tomorrow and all the days to come? Would she ever see him again?

Hurriedly she knelt down and, putting her head into the mouth of the hole, shouted, "Paddy! Paddy! There's something I must ask you!"

But there was no answer.

CHAPTER 4

At the Pigsties

"What's the matter, Brigid?" said Mother at lunchtime. "You've hardly touched your food."

"Ate too much for breakfast, I expect," Dada said. "Or is it that birthday cake at teatime you're thinking about?"

"I feel a bit sick," Brigid said. Sick with worry, she thought. Suppose I can't ever see Paddy again! That would be *awful*. Imagine knowing he's down there in the badgers' set or talking to Fillpail or Snowy or Neddy or having a discussion with the pigs and not being able to see him—or hear him, I suppose.

Mother put the flat of her hand against Brigid's forehead.

"You don't feel feverish," she said. "You'd better leave the table and sit quietly somewhere for a while. Read your new animal encyclopedia."

Brigid looked in the book, just in case it might say something about leprechauns, but there was nothing between "leopard" and "leveret."

Well, there wouldn't be, silly, she said to herself. Leps aren't animals, they're people—little people, little emerald people.

She looked at her watch. It had been noon when Paddy had gone for his nap. Now it was getting on two o'clock. Surely that would be long enough for him?

"I feel all right now, Mother," Brigid said. "I'm going out."

"If you're all right, you're well enough to help with the dishes," said Mother. "And after that, I have a job for you. I know it's the holidays, but you've plenty of time for play, and a little work won't hurt you. My vegetable garden's as full of weeds as an egg is of yolk. You can do an hour or so's weeding for me."

"But it's my birthday."

"Dishes don't clean themselves nor weeds jump out of the ground because of that."

The dishes were soon done, but the "hour or so's" weeding took longer because Mother came to lend a hand and kept saying, "We'll just do this little patch and that little patch," so that it was four o'clock before Brigid was free.

Once out of sight of the house and the farm buildings, she ran like a stag for the wood. At the set there was silence, broken only by tiny snapping noises as a few leaves fell from the trees. It was hard to believe that some-

where under her feet as she stood on the tump were a whole family of badgers and an old leprechaun. Was he still asleep? Or had he woken and gone out again?

He'll have left tracks, thought Brigid, and she began to examine the ground.

The recent rain had made it muddy, and she could easily see the tread marks of her boots and the very small prints made by the leprechaun's frog-skin ones, though it was difficult to see which way these were pointing.

Then she saw that just outside Paddy's front entrance a picture had been drawn in the mud with a stick. It was a picture of a fat pig with floppy ears and a curly tail—there was no mistaking it.

I don't suppose he's ever learned to read and write, thought Brigid as she raced back, but he draws beautifully.

As she neared the pigsties she heard a good deal of grunting coming from one of them and saw a curl of blue smoke rising. Sure enough, there was P.V.W.R.H. O'Reilly sitting on a pigsty wall with his little green legs dangling, puffing on his nose warmer, while beneath him half a dozen porkers stood looking up.

"Ah, there you are, Brigid!" he said after taking the pipe out of his mouth and grinning his crinkly grin. "You got my message, then?"

"Oh, yes," panted Brigid, "but Paddy, there's something I must ask you!"

"Is it money you're wanting to borrow again?" said Paddy.

"No, no, it's something terribly important. Will I *see* you tomorrow?"

"I imagine so. Unless you're going away— to England or America or some such outlandish place. I shall be here, as I have been these last one hundred and seventy-four years."

"No, I mean—will I be *able* to see you? When my birthday's over? You said people could only see a lep *on* their birthday. Oh, Paddy, I couldn't bear it if you're just going to vanish after today," said Brigid, her gray eyes filling with tears.

Paddy put out a hand. He would have held

hers, but it was too big, so he held her little finger.

"There, there, dear girl," he said. "Don't be getting yourself into a state. You've nothing to worry about. It's only to see a lep in the first place that it must be your birthday and all those other things. After all, you're not going to have a hole in your boot forever. Which reminds me, I must mend it. No, no, now that you've seen me, you'll always be able to, so long as I live."

"Oh, Paddy, I am glad," said Brigid, wiping her eyes. She would have liked to have given him a big hug, but he was too little, so she contented herself by gently stroking his red hair.

The porkers commenced to grunt again, having, she supposed, a lot more things to discuss with the leprechaun, but then she suddenly thought of what he had just said to her. "So long as I live," he had said.

The relief that she would always be able to see him was replaced by this new and awful worry. After all, he had been hatched in the year of Waterloo! But perhaps leps, like old soldiers, never die but simply fade away?

She decided to approach the subject in a roundabout way.

"It's funny to think," she said, leaning on the pigsty wall beside Paddy and looking down, "that I'm eight years old, but these porkers aren't even eight months old."

Paddy cupped his mouth with his hand and spoke softly into her ear.

"They never will be," he said.

"You mean . . . ?"

"The butcher, yes."

"Oh, dear," said Brigid, "but everyone has to die sometime, I suppose."

"They do, they do."

"Even leps?"

"Even leps, dear girl. We have long lives, so we do, long and happy lives, but all good things must come to an end," said Paddy.

Brigid took a deep breath.

"How long *do* leps live?" she asked.

"Oh, about twice as long as the average human," said P.V.W.R.H. O'Reilly.

For a while neither spoke.

The leprechaun was smoking his pipe, puffing away contentedly and blowing out little clouds of blue smoke, while Brigid was doing arithmetic in her head as best she could.

How long did the average human live? Three-score years and ten, it said in the Bible. That was seventy. $70 \times 2 = 140$. But Paddy was already one hundred and seventy-four! Half of one hundred and seventy-four was . . . let's see . . . eighty-seven. He was already eighty-seven in human terms! But then some people lived to be one hundred. That would be two hundred in a lep. So he might have . . . um . . . er . . . twenty-six years of life left yet. By then she would be $8 + 26 = 34$! Perhaps she didn't have to worry.

Then she saw something that started her worrying like mad. There was Dada coming across the yard with a bucket of pig mash in either hand, and the porkers, smelling it, began to squeal.

"Quick, Paddy!" she whispered. "Dada's coming, he'll see you!"

"He will not," said Paddy, puffing away.

"But then he'll see the smoke from your pipe!"

"He will not. He cannot see me, nor my pipe, nor the smoke from it. Because he cannot see me, he cannot hear what I say either. Just you watch."

"Talking to the pigs, Brigid?" said Dada as he came up and set down the buckets to open the sty door.

"Yes, Dada," said Brigid.

"YES, DADA!" shouted Paddy at the top of his voice.

Dada took not the slightest bit of notice. He carried the buckets into the sty and poured the warm slop of barley meal and flaked corn and cooked small potatoes into the trough for the jostling porkers.

While he was doing this, Paddy knocked out his pipe and, putting it into his tunic pocket, stood up and began to do a little dance on top of the pigsty wall. As he danced he sang a little song.

"My name is O'Reilly,
I'm witty, I'm wily,
I dance with the daintiest steps.
No other O'Reilly
Is thought of so highly
As Patrick, the pride of the leps."

He sang this at the top of his voice, leaping and capering like a dervish, but Dada simply picked up the empty pails, closed and bolted the sty door, and went off back across the yard, saying as he did so, "Time for our tea soon, Brigid. I'm looking forward to a piece of that birthday cake that Mother's made you!"

"You see," said Paddy. "Never saw a thing, never heard a thing."

"But all the animals can?"

"Sure, all the animals can."

"What were you talking about to the pigs?"

"You."

"Me?"

"Yes, I was telling them what a nice little girl you are—big girl, I suppose I should say—and how it was your birthday and how your mother had made you a grand cake and how—after your tea—you were going to bring the dearest wee slice of it—just a smidgen, with maybe a nice bit of the icing and the marzipan in it—to your friend P.V.W.R.H. O'Reilly," said Paddy, and he set to dancing once again, singing his little song.

CHAPTER 5

Behind the Chicken House

"There's something the matter with the don-key," said Dada at breakfast the next morning. "He doesn't have much appetite these days, no interest in his food. He's beginning to look quite ribby."

"Poor Neddy," said Mother. "Of course he's quite old—he must be twenty-five, because I got him as a foal when I was about Brigid's age."

"I can't make out what's wrong with him," said Dada. "That's the trouble with animals. They can't tell you what the matter is. If only he could."

Brigid said nothing, but after breakfast she set off for the wood. If Paddy was at home, she knew now how to attract his attention. They had talked about it at the pigsties.

"I shouted down the hole," Brigid had said, "but you didn't hear."

"The tunnel twists and turns," Paddy had

said. "It shuts the sound out. You want to do what people do on your front door—knock."

"But you haven't got a front door."

"Knock on the trunk of the elder tree that stands above," Paddy had said. "I can feel the vibrations down the roots. Wake me from the deepest sleep, that will."

So now Brigid found a stout stick and banged on the trunk of the elder, and after a few moments Paddy came out of his hole yawning and knuckling his eyes, which looked bleary. The end of his nose, Brigid noticed, was unusually red.

"Oh, dear!" she said. "Did I wake you?"

"Just having a little sleep-in, I was," said Paddy. "That's the trouble with my landlords being nocturnal folk. Made a bit of a night of it, I did."

"You mean you sat up late talking to the badgers?"

"Talking, yes."

"And smoking that nose warmer of yours too much, I suppose?"

"Ah, it wasn't the smoking," said Paddy.

"Maybe I had a drop too much taken."

"Paddy! You've been drinking?"

"Well, now, every lep likes a drink, you know. A pipe and a nice drop, and you have a happy lep."

"What sort of drink?"

"Ah, now, whiskey is the greatest drink, but that's not so easy to get hold of. So I brew my own ale. Heather ale it is, made from the tops of the heather, and a tankard or two of that makes a new lep of me. But maybe last night it was more like a tankard or five or six," said Paddy, and he held both hands to his head as though he feared it might fall apart.

"Why did you drink such a lot?" asked Brigid.

"Wasn't I celebrating?"

"Celebrating what?"

"Why, celebrating meeting you, dear girl," said Paddy.

The sight of the leprechaun looking so poorly reminded Brigid of why she needed his help.

"Paddy," she said, "do you feel well enough to come to the farm with me?"

" 'Tis a long walk for me," said Paddy doubtfully. "My legs are not themselves this morning."

"I could carry you," said Brigid. "If you wouldn't mind. You see, Neddy's not at all well, and I'd be ever so grateful if you could have a talk with him and find out what the matter is. Dada and Mother are worried about him. It will only take a minute and then I'll bring you straight back and you can go to bed until you're feeling better. Please, Paddy!"

"Ah, well, seeing it's the old donkey that's in trouble, and you asking so nicely," said the leprechaun, and he held out his arms to be lifted up.

Neddy was standing in the corner of the orchard looking listless. Brigid picked up a fallen apple, something she knew he liked, and offered it, but the donkey turned his head away.

"Hold me up so that I can speak into his great old ear, Brigid," said Paddy. And when she did, he said, "What's the matter with you, my friend?"

For an answer Neddy stretched out his neck and gave a long creaking heehawing bray, as melancholy a sound as you could imagine.

Paddy listened carefully to this noise and then said, "Ah, so that's the trouble."

"What?" said Brigid. "What is it?"

"It's his teeth," said Paddy. "He's old, you see, and so are his teeth, and they've gotten rough, with sharp edges here and there that make it difficult and painful for him to chew. That's why he's off his food—he can't chew it properly."

"What can we do? What can Dada do?"

"Why, get the horse doctor. He'll file the rough parts down, and then Neddy will be as right as rain. And now take me home, there's a dear, and maybe I'll have a little nap."

When Brigid returned from the badgers' set, she went to find Dada.

"Dada," she said, "aren't you going to get the horse doctor to have a look at Neddy?"

"All in good time," Dada said.

PADDY'S POT OF GOLD

At lunch Mother said to him, "Aren't you going to get the horse doctor to have a look at Neddy?"

"All in good time," Dada said.

"Now, look," said Mother, and she said it firmly, for she knew how long it took Dada to get around to mowing the lawn or mending the farmyard gate or putting back the shingles that had blown off the cowshed roof or a hundred and one other things that he was going to do, all in good time. "Now, look. Neddy is *my* donkey, and *I* want the horse doctor to see him."

Brigid had never met the horse doctor before, and when he arrived that afternoon she thought she had seldom seen such an odd-looking little man (excepting P.V.W.R.H. O'Reilly). He was small, a head shorter than Dada, with thin legs so bowed that a good-size pig could easily have run through them, and his clothes looked as though they had all been made from horse skin—and the skin of a dirty old brown pony at that. Over his shoulder he carried a bag filled with bottles of medicines for

treating horses' stomachs and tools such as files
and paring knives for dealing with their hoofs.

He stood and looked at Neddy.

"And what's the matter with the old donkey?" he said.

"He won't eat," said Dada. "He's not interested in his food."

The horse doctor prodded Neddy in the stomach.

"It's the colic," he said. "No doubt about it. He needs a drench. I have just the thing for it." And he drew from his bag a large bottle filled with a thick mud-colored medicine.

Poor Neddy, thought Brigid, having to drink that muck.

"Excuse me," she said politely. "I don't think it's his stomach that's the trouble."

The horse doctor stopped in the act of drawing the cork from his bottle and looked at her.

"Hush, Brigid," said Dada. "The man's an expert."

"How old are you, child?" said the horse doctor.

"I'm eight."

"Eight, is it? And there's me fifty-eight and doctoring every horse and pony and donkey in the county of Cork, but the child knows better than me, I suppose."

I do, said Brigid to herself.

"Tell us, then, child," said the horse doctor. "What ails the donkey that he won't eat?"

"I think," said Brigid carefully, "it's more that he *can't* eat. He'd like to, but it's too painful. It's his teeth, I think."

The horse doctor shook his head, smiling.

"His teeth, is it?" he said, winking at Dada. "Maybe he needs a set of false ones."

He opened the donkey's jaws and peered in. Then, Brigid saw, his own jaw dropped.

"Just as I thought," he said hastily. "Indeed it is his teeth. All sharp edges the old things are, cutting his gums and his tongue, poor beast, when he tries to eat."

"What can you do for him?" said Dada.

"Why, I'll file them down," said the horse doctor. "I'll take off all the sharp edges and he'll be able to chew away to his heart's content."

He reached into his bag and brought out a file.

"That's a smart little girl you have there," he said. "I was just about to suggest a look in the old donkey's mouth, but she was too quick for me."

"That was clever of you, Brigid," said Dada

when the horse doctor had gone. "I don't know how you guessed the trouble with Neddy."

"Something just told me what it was," said Brigid.

The favor done to Neddy was only the first of many services that the leprechaun was able to render. Because he was forever having "a good chitchat" with one or another of the animals, Brigid was now aware of everything that was going on at the farm in a way that neither Dada nor Mother nor any other human being could possibly have been. If Fillpail the cow or one of the pigs or any of the poultry were a bit unwell, Paddy would hear of it and tell Brigid, and Brigid would draw Dada's attention to the matter.

"Suddenly she has a wonderful eye for the livestock," Dada told Mother. "She seems to know instinctively when an animal's not right."

And indeed she was once able to prevent a great tragedy.

As she went early one morning to roll back Snowy's sack curtain, a curl of smoke rising near his hutch told her that Paddy was already waiting for her. Surprised, because he was not as a rule the earliest of risers, she ran across the garden to find him walking to and fro in a nervous manner, puffing furiously at his nose warmer.

"Paddy!" she said. "What's the matter?"

"Ah, there you are!" cried the leprechaun. "And not a moment too soon!"

"Why? What has happened?"

Paddy did not answer. Instead he said, "Has your dada let the hens out of the chicken house yet?"

"No, not yet. He's milking Fillpail."

"You must stop him."

"Stop him from milking Fillpail?"

"No, no. Stop him from letting out the birds."

"But why?"

"I'll tell you, Brigid. Last evening I was down at the end of the wood picking a few blackberries—from the lowest branches, you understand—when I smelled a nasty old smell."

"A fox?" said Brigid.

"Two of them," said Paddy, "curled up in-side the blackberry thicket. Now, a man of my size is not all that keen on meeting one fox, let alone a couple, so I was just about to slip away home when they started talking.

" 'When the man has milked the cow,' says the one, 'that's when he lets them out.'

" 'Then what?' says the other.

" 'He feeds them, and he feeds the pigs.'

" 'Where's the woman?'

" 'In the house.'

" 'And the child?'

" 'Goes across the garden to feed her rabbit. Put a sack over his hutch at nights, she has. Pity. I used to enjoy staring at him.'

" 'And then?'

" 'The child goes back into the house, and the man, too. There's no one about for half an hour or more.'

" 'Half an hour's plenty of time. We could kill a good many hens in half an hour.'

" 'We could kill *all* of them,' says the one.

" 'Tomorrow, then,' says the other.

"So you see, Brigid, there'll be a massacre

this morning unless you can stop it. Has your dada got a gun?"

"Yes. But Paddy, I can't say 'Dada, don't let the hens out, or if you do, don't go into the house—hide, with your gun ready.' He'd say 'Why?' And I'd have to say 'There's two foxes coming this breakfast time to kill all our hens.' And he'd say 'How do you know?' And I'd have to say 'A leprechaun told me.' I can't do that, can I?"

Paddy thought for a moment.

"Tell him you dreamed it," he said. "A very vivid dream it was, say. Off you go quick now, but put me up on top of Snowy's hutch first so's I can see the fun."

And he sat happily smoking his pipe and watched Brigid run to the cowshed and after a while Dada go to the house for his gun and come back and let out the hens and then hide.

There were others hiding, too, and soon two low red shapes came out of the wood and trotted across the field as bold as brass and slipped under the gate and into the yard where the big flock

of brown and white and speckled hens strutted and scratched and clucked and pecked.

Shoulder to shoulder the two foxes stood, their eyes fixed gloatingly on the birds, their minds filled with thoughts of the feast to come.

"Now, Dada, now!" said P.V.W.R.H. O'Reilly softly, and as though in obedience to his orders, Dada's old gun roared out.

"Did you see, Paddy?" said Brigid afterward, when she came to lift him down from the top of the hutch. "They won't come back in a hurry!"

"Indeed they won't," said Paddy. "A pity it is that they weren't killed entirely, but your dada gave them a good peppering. Lead it was they had for breakfast, not chicken."

"Oh, Paddy," said Brigid, "if Dada only knew! I shall get the praise, but it was you who saved our hens. The foxes would have killed them all, and think what it would have cost Dada to buy new ones. He hasn't a great deal of money, you know."

But you have, she couldn't stop herself from thinking. You have a pot of gold buried somewhere. But I shall never ask you about it, never. You're my friend.

"Think nothing of it, dear girl," said Paddy. "I'm your friend. And who knows, one of these days maybe you'll be able to do me a favor in return."

CHAPTER 6

At the Set

"It's hard to believe," said Mother to Dada after Brigid had gone to school. "First she knew what was wrong with Neddy. Then she seems to know instinctively when any of the animals is sick or needs anything. And now she goes and has a dream and it comes true."

"I told her not to be so silly, just now when she came into the cowshed," Dada said, "but she kept on and she sounded so desperate about it that in the end I went and fetched the gun, and a good thing too! They won't come back in a hurry!"

"But it's very strange, you must admit," said Mother. "And all these things have happened since her birthday. Anyone would think she was in league with the little people."

"Ah, come on, now!"

"You told her you believed in them."

"Ah, well, it's one thing to say to a child . . .

Anyway, you went on about leprechauns and pots of gold—you're as bad as I am!"

They looked at each other and laughed rather self-consciously.

At school that day Brigid's mind was not on her work. It was full of an idea she had had. Always she had wanted to see a badger, yet never in all her eight years had she been able to. Quite often she had gone to the wood at dusk, hoping that they would come out, until she heard Mother's voice calling her home. But they never had.

That was before she had met Paddy. Now, surely, he would be able to arrange something with his landlords. He could reassure them, tell them they'd be in no danger, that she only wanted to see them, nothing more.

And when her teacher said suddenly, in a math lesson, "And what was I just talking about, Brigid?" she replied "Badgers," and everyone roared with laughter.

Home again, she slipped away to the wood as soon as she could. It was very silent, the only sounds the rustle of her feet through the fallen leaves and the melancholy singing of a robin. She climbed the tump and banged on the elder tree.

Paddy came out of his hole. He was wearing a little leather apron (green, of course), and he had a tiny cobbler's hammer in his (right) hand. He did not answer at first when Brigid spoke to him, and she saw that he held a number of tacks between his lips.

"Sorry," said Brigid. "I'm interrupting your work."

Paddy took the tacks out of his mouth.

"That reminds me," he said. "I told you I'd mend that old boot of yours and I've never done it. Take it off. I'll do it now."

"But Paddy, I wanted to ask you something," said Brigid, taking off her boot.

"In a minute. It won't take me a minute," said the leprechaun.

Brigid sat on a fallen elder branch, thinking of Paddy working away six feet below her, when suddenly she heard someone whistling a tune. It was Dada, collecting firewood, something he loved doing.

At the Set

He mustn't see me, thought Brigid. She was allowed in the wood, of course—Dada knew she was interested in the badgers—and normally she would have called to him and run to join him. But not with only one boot on! What would he think!

Quickly she slid down the far side of the tump, and jammed herself feet first into the mouth of the biggest of all the badgers' entrances. If Dada does find me, she thought quickly, I'll say I was hiding for fun. But what about the missing boot? It fell down the badgers' hole, that's what.

She waited breathlessly, eyes closed. The whistling had stopped.

Then, suddenly and very close, she heard a familiar cackling laugh, like the cry of the green woodpecker. She looked up to see Paddy. For once he was looking down at her.

"There's a sight!" he spluttered. "Here's your boot. I've patched it, put it on, what, d'you want to be, a badger?"

"No, but I want to *see* a badger," said Brigid, pulling herself out of the hole and pulling

66

the boot onto her foot. "Could you arrange it for me, Paddy? I've never seen one."

"Nothing easier," said Paddy.

He looked up at the sky, where the light was just beginning to fade.

"They'll be out now in half an hour, or they would be if you weren't here. I'll have a word with them. Come you back this time tomorrow. Off you go now and leave it all to me."

"Oh, thank you, Paddy," said Brigid. "And thank you for mending my boot."

I can't think how he did it, she said to herself as she went home. The boot's rubber. Maybe he stuck on some frog skin and painted it black. In the yard she climbed into the cattle trough and stood in it to test the boot, and not a drop of water came in.

As she approached the set the following evening she could see first the smoke from the leprechaun's pipe and then the little man himself, sitting on the fallen branch. In his (right) hand he held a very small tankard, cleverly made from wood, with a beautifully carved tiny handle in the shape of a caterpillar. He raised it when he saw her and with a cry of "Slainte!" drank her health. Brigid looked anxiously at his nose, but it was only faintly rosy.

"Would you be wanting to try a drop of my heather ale, dear girl?" he asked.

"No, thank you," said Brigid. "I'm not old enough."

"Praise be," said Paddy, "I am."

"Did you speak to your landlords?" Brigid asked.

"I did. They have no objection, seeing as you're a friend of mine, but of course you are also a human being and they're normally suspicious of human beings, so you must be still and silent. Sit here and don't move," said Paddy, and he drained his tankard and hopped off the branch.

"Where are you going?" said Brigid. "Aren't you going to stay with me?"

"There's something I need from my storeroom," said Paddy. "I'll be back in two shakes of a duck's tail." And he dived down his hole.

He was back in a few moments with a full tankard and a pleased look, and he clambered up to sit beside her.

Now began for Brigid a magical time, a time she was to remember all her life. It was a still dry windless autumn evening after a still dry windless autumn day, and soon, while there was still plenty of light to see by, the badgers began to come out of the set.

Brigid did not notice the first one till Paddy
nudged her, and then she saw, in the mouth of
one of the biggest holes, a head looking out. A
broad, powerful head it was, with two black
stripes running from each short ear down over
each eye to the muzzle, and a broad white stripe
between.

The head was raised to sniff the evening air.
Then it turned so that the dark eyes looked
straight at her.

"That's the old boar," said Paddy very
softly. "Don't move now. He'll come out
soon."

And in a minute the boar badger emerged
and walked down the side of the tump with a
slow, rolling bearlike shuffle. And then out after
him came the sow and no less than five cubs,
perfect small copies of their parents.

"Born in the early summer," said Paddy.
"Isn't it a grand lot they are?" And he raised his
tankard to the watching badgers and took a
drink of his heather ale.

Brigid sat motionless, enthralled. In a few
seconds they'll be gone, I suppose, she thought,

but at least now I've seen a whole family of badgers.

But the badgers seemed in no hurry to begin their night's hunting. The adults snuffled about among the leaves and rolled and scratched themselves, and the cubs began to play, tumbling one another over in mock fights with loud clucking noises of pleasure. So absorbed were they in their fun that two of them, playing king of the hill, ran up over Brigid's feet before skidding back down the side of the tump again.

"Are these all the badgers in the set?" she whispered.

"No, no," said Paddy. "There's three families altogether. They'll all be out in a minute."

And sure enough, on that enchanted evening, Brigid was to see no less than six adults and a dozen cubs of various sizes, all now joining in greeting and play, all seemingly unafraid and confident in her presence.

Then at last, as the light began to fade, a distant voice suddenly called, "Brigid! Brigid! Time to come in now." And before you could say "P.V.W.R.H. O'Reilly," there wasn't a badger to be seen.

Brigid stood up and stretched.

"Oh, that was lovely!" she sighed, and she smiled and set off for home.

The leprechaun drained his tankard.

"Oh, that was lovely!" he said, and he grinned and scuttled down his hole.

CHAPTER 7

In the Supermarket

Autumn, to no one's surprise, turned into winter, but winter, to Brigid's surprise, meant that she saw a great deal less of P.V.W.R.H. O'Reilly.

It wasn't particularly because she was at school or because the days were so much shorter. It just seemed that now he needed an awful lot of sleep, by day as well as by night, and she seldom met him about the farm.

Then there was a sudden cold snap, and though she went to the set and banged on the elder tree, there was no response. Day after day she banged with her banging stick, but no little green-faced red-headed figure came out of the hole.

Maybe he's out all the time, she thought, and she went to Snowy, to Neddy, to Fillpail, and to the pigs and asked them if they had seen him. But of course though they replied with an assortment of noises, she got no information.

He could communicate with them, she could not.

As if to underline his absence, two of the hens took sick and, with no Paddy to draw Brigid's attention to their state of health, turned up their toes and died.

Then came the first fall of snow. It was only an inch or so, but enough to prove to Brigid, searching the whitened tump for tracks and finding only the badgers' and her own, that no one wearing frog-skin boots was going in or out of a particular hole.

That night she lay in bed thinking. Could she have lost the gift of seeing the leprechaun? Maybe he was around all the time, but she could no longer see him or his pipe smoke or his tracks or hear his voice or his cackling laugh. Would she have to wait until her next birthday (and make a fresh hole in her boot)? No, no, that couldn't be the answer. She remembered his exact words: "Now that you've seen me, you'll always be able to . . ." And then she caught her breath at the memory of what came next: ". . . so long as I live."

"Oh, no," said Brigid in a small, miserable voice, "he couldn't be . . ."

But he could. He was so old. She buried her face in the pillow.

In the night the weather changed completely and the snow vanished. Brigid woke convinced that she had seen the last of P.V.W.R.H. O'Reilly.

"What's the matter?" Mother said at breakfast. "You've a face as long as Neddy's."

"Cheer up," said Dada. "Look, the sun's shining. It's going to be a lovely day."

"Oh, Snowy," said Brigid as she fed her rabbit when she came back from school that afternoon, "what shall I do?"

For an answer the white buck rabbit banged hard with his hind feet on the floorboards of the hutch.

Brigid looked at him, then shut the hutch door and turned and ran for the wood. It was indeed a lovely day, and in the bare branches of the trees a few birds were singing uncertainly in the mild sunshine, deceived into thinking that spring had come.

Brigid scrambled up the side of the tump, picked up her banging stick, and in one last frenzy of desperation began to beat the elder tree with all her strength.

At last she stopped and leaned against the trunk of the tree, panting. The birds had fallen silent, and the wood was still.

Then a voice said, "Brigid, Brigid, what a racket! Why, it's enough to wake the dead!" And there at the mouth of his hole stood a very sleepy-looking leprechaun. His red hair was tousled, and his green clothes were covered in leaves and bracken fronds and very rumpled.

"Oh, Paddy, Paddy!" cried Brigid, swoop-

ing on him and lifting him high. "Where have you been?"

"In bed."

"But why?"

"To sleep. Do you not go to bed to sleep?"

"But I haven't seen you for a whole month. D'you mean you've been fast asleep all that time?"

"I do."

"You've been hibernating!"

"You have it entirely. Put me down now, dear girl. Isn't it giddy you're making me, shaking me and squeezing me like that."

"Oh, Paddy, I've been so worried!" said Brigid, setting him down. "I couldn't find you anywhere, and I couldn't make you hear, and I thought . . . Oh, Paddy, it's lovely to see you again, and the sun's shining, and I feel so happy, and it'll soon be Christmas . . . Oh, what would you like for Christmas?"

"Something to keep the cold out," said Paddy.

"A coat? A blanket?"

"I was thinking more of the inner man."

"The inner man?"

"My little inside. A wee drop. To warm me."

"Whiskey, you mean?"

"You have it entirely. John Jameson or Bushmills. I'm not fussy."

"A whole bottle?" said Brigid doubtfully.

"Oh, bless you, now, I was thinking of a miniature—you can buy them in the supermarket, you know. But I'm only joking, Brigid. You mustn't be bothering with a Christmas present for me. I've nothing to give you in return."

He took out his little green purse and opened it and peered in.

"Sorry," he said. "I've only got one shilling. 'Tis all I have in the world."

Brigid ran home as happy as could be, skipping like a lamb and singing like a lark.

"You've changed your tune," said Mother at suppertime. "You look like the cat that's eaten the cream."

"You see," said Dada. "I told you it would be a lovely day."

PADDY'S POT OF GOLD

"Oh, Snowy," said Brigid, lifting his sack curtain to have a last good night look at him, "it *has* been a lovely day."

Snowy made no answer, but his pink eyes glowed warmly in the light of the rising moon.

It was some days later, with Christmas now fast approaching, that Brigid went to buy Paddy's present. She had thought it all out. She would go to the supermarket with Mother and Dada, and then, telling them that she wanted to buy presents for them in secret and making them promise not to look, she would arrange to meet them outside.

"Don't wait by the checkout counter," she said, "or you'll see what I've got."

She did indeed intend to buy them presents as well as Paddy. She just hoped she'd have enough money left for that miniature bottle of whiskey.

She bought Mother a box of milk chocolates and Dada a pen that wrote in six different colors (both things she would have liked for herself— Brigid's way of selecting presents).

Then, making sure that they were not

watching, she went to the liquor counter. There she found a wire basket piled high with miniature bottles of drinks of all kinds—gin, vodka, rum, brandy, Scotch whisky, and many others. But she could not find one that carried the name of either Mr. John Jameson's or Mr. Bushmills' Irish whiskey. What should she do? Would Scotch whisky be all right for Paddy?

At last, to her relief, she saw a little bottle labeled Baileys Original Irish Cream. Cream? Well, it looked like whiskey. But could she afford it? She had one pound left. She looked at the price tag: seventy-two pence. She put the bottle in her basket and went to the checkout.

The checkout clerk rang up the chocolates and the pen and then held up the miniature.

"What's this, little girl?" she said.

"It says 'Cream,' " said Brigid.

"It's Irish whiskey, is this," said the checkout clerk. "I can't sell this to a little girl like you, now can I?"

"But it's not for me. It's for—" began Brigid, and then stopped. She was a truthful child and could not quite bring herself to say "It's for my dada," when it wasn't.

"It's for your dada!" said the checkout clerk. "Isn't that right?" And before Brigid was forced to answer, she went on. "I thought it was, and there's the lucky man he is. Ah, well, all right, then, seeing it's nearly Christmastime and me knowing you're a truthful little girl by the look of you, aren't you?"

Brigid nodded, and the clerk rang up the miniature and took the money, and Brigid put the three presents in her bag.

Home again, she wrapped them carefully, labeled them, and hid them under a loose floorboard in her bedroom. Each morning now she counted the days till Christmas. Would it be a white one? she wondered. Would Paddy be back in hibernation again? Perhaps she had better give him his present early.

On the first day of the holidays she put the wrapped bottle in her pocket and set out for the wood, only to notice, as she went across the garden, a familiar curl of blue smoke rising—in the cowshed this time. She found Paddy lying comfortably in the soft hay of Fillpail's stall, puffing at his nose warmer.

"The old cow's been telling me," he said, "she has a touch of foul-in-the-foot."

"What's that?" said Brigid.

"A bit of an infection in her hoof. The right hind foot it is. 'Tis swollen and painful to walk on."

"I'll tell Dada," said Brigid.

"And he'll do something about it 'all in good time,' " said Paddy, grinning wickedly.

"Now, now, Paddy," said Brigid. "Don't you say such things about my dada, or I won't give you your Christmas present."

"Have you got it, then?"

"I have it with me now. I was going to bring it to your lodgings," said Brigid, and she reached into her pocket and brought out the little bottle-shaped parcel in its colored paper and with its label around its neck.

"You mustn't open it until Christmas Day," she said.

"Would I do such a thing?" said Paddy.

"Tell me, Brigid," he said. "What does it say on the label?"

Silly me, thought Brigid, I'd forgotten. He probably can't read.

"I never had any schooling, you see," said Paddy. "What have you written on it?"

"It says 'A merry Christmas and a happy New Year to P.V.W.R.H. O'Reilly, Esquire, with love from Brigid.' "

"There's a dear girl you are," said Paddy. "I shall drink to your health on the day and wish you a long life."

"It won't be as long as yours," said Brigid, laughing.

"No, but it will be a happy one, I hope. You're happy now, are you not?"

"I am."

"So you should be, living in this beautiful part of old Ireland, with a mother and dada like yours, and with all these animals to tend to, like old Fillpail here."

He stretched out a little green arm and gently scratched the cow's velvety muzzle with his green fingernails. In return she blew a long,

In the Supermarket

sweet hay breath at him, making the smoke from his pipe dance and jiggle in the dust-filled air.

"In fact," said Paddy, "there's nothing you lack, I should imagine."

PADDY'S POT OF GOLD

"Only money, I suppose," said Brigid. "We're quite poor, you know. I don't mind for myself, but it would be nice for Mother to have new things for the house and for Dada to afford another cow or two, perhaps. I wish I could help. But I won't be old enough to earn money for a long time."

"Maybe you'll find some," said Paddy in an offhand way.

"Find some?"

"Buried treasure—that sort of thing."

Like that pot of gold you have buried some-where, Brigid could not stop herself from think-ing, and suddenly she felt sour. I'll never ask him, but if I did, he'd never tell me. He's mean, like all leps are, and he's a miser, too. "Only one shilling" indeed! And what good is the gold to him? He pays no rent to the badgers, he takes the tops off Dada's heather for his ale, he steals Dada's seaweed for his tobacco and what veg-etables he fancies, I suppose, and he'll swig down that whiskey that cost me seventy-two pence, and will I ever get anything in return? Never!

And then, just as suddenly, she felt ashamed

85

of her thoughts—about her friend at that, especially because she felt, as she often did, that
maybe he could read them as he sat watching
her with his twinkling green eyes.

"What are you thinking?" she asked.

The leprechaun gave his cackling laugh.

"I was thinking," he said, "what a generous
girl you are, spending your precious pocket
money buying me a grand Christmas present.
And what do you get in return? Nothing! What
a mean old lep he is, you must be thinking."

"Oh, no, oh, dear," said Brigid in confu-
sion. "I don't want . . . I don't expect anything
from you, Paddy. Just your friendship, that's
all."

"And that you will have, dear girl," said
P.V.W.R.H. O'Reilly, "until my dying day."

CHAPTER 8

In the Wood

The miniature whiskey bottle, which stood perhaps a third of Paddy's height, would have been
an awkward burden for Paddy to carry back
home, so Brigid offered to carry it for him.

"That's kind of you," he said, "and if you
cared to give me a lift as well, I wouldn't say
no. The old legs get tired easily these days."

Before, Brigid had carried him in her arms
like a doll, but that seemed somehow undigni-
fied. She was wondering how best to go about
it when Paddy said, "Piggyback, if you please."

So she hoisted him up, and he sat at the back
of her neck like a tiny jockey, his green legs
crossed under her chin.

"Can I hold your ears to balance meself?" he
asked, and she nodded.

"There's lovely dark hair you have," said
Paddy, "and the gray eyes and the freckles. Isn't
it the proper colleen you are!"

"You've a wonderful head of hair, Paddy,"

said Brigid. "Such a bright red it is, and not a gray hair to be seen."

"You'll never see a gray-haired lep," he said. "Nor a bald one. And you'll not see a bearded lep either. 'Tis only our heads that are thatched, to keep the Irish rain out."

When they came to the set, Brigid lifted the leprechaun off her shoulders and set him down by his hole. She took the bottle-shaped parcel from her pocket and gave it to him.

"Can you manage it?" she said.

"With the greatest of ease, dear girl," said Paddy. "It'll roll down the hole as easy as the contents will slip down me throat. And I thank you again for your kindness. Give us your finger now."

Brigid held out one finger and Paddy shook it.

"Will I see you on Christmas Day?" he said.

"Oh, yes," said Brigid. "Unless the weather turns cold and you've gone to sleep again."

"It'll stay mild till the new year, so my land-lords tell me," said Paddy, "and then there's a big freeze coming. Badgers have a great nose for the weather."

Paddy's nose, when Brigid saw him on Christmas Day, was a delicate shade of rose. He was in patently high spirits, singing more loudly and dancing less surefootedly than usual and laughing his cackling laugh like the cry of the green woodpecker.

But the next day it was a very different story.

It took a great deal of effort with the banging stick to fetch him from his hole, and when at

last he did come out, he was exceedingly grumpy.

"Leave off, do!" he growled at Brigid, holding his head in his hands. "Give a poor lep a bit of peace, can't you?"

"There's no need to bite my head off," said Brigid in a hurt voice.

Little did she know that before the day was out, it would be Paddy's head that would be in grave danger of being bitten off.

That afternoon Brigid went for a walk. Automatically she was heading for the wood, but then she thought she had no wish to be snubbed again. She was about to turn back when she saw a low red shape slinking along the hedge. The fox—it was lame, she could see—slipped in among the trees, and Brigid ran for home.

"Dada!" she panted when she found him. "The fox! One of the ones you shot—he was limping. He's at the bottom edge of the wood now!"

"Run up the hill," said Dada, "and get be-

hind the wood on the top side to stop him from breaking that way! I'll get the old gun!"

That afternoon P.V.W.R.H. O'Reilly went for a walk. He thought the fresh air would do him good. He was also not at all pleased with himself for having snapped at Brigid. Later, he thought, he would find her to say he was sorry, but for now he turned his back on the farm and walked through the wood. He was nearing the far edge near the top when he heard a voice behind him.

"I wonder if you could spare me a moment," said the fox. He wrinkled his lips in what might have been a smile. It seemed to Paddy that the fox had a great many sharp teeth.

"I'm in a bit of a hurry," said Paddy hastily.

"Ah, this won't take long," said the fox easily. "I just wanted to pick your brains."

"Pick my . . . ?"

"Yes, you see, my brother and I, a while back, were planning a little raid. On the farmer's chickens, you understand? It went wrong. Somebody grassed on us."

"Grassed?"

"Sneaked. Gave the game away. Sold us down the river."

"Who would do such a terrible thing?" said Paddy.

"I wonder," said the fox softly. "Could it be somebody who heard us talking? And that somebody told the child, and the child told the man, and the man fired the gun. Myself, I was lucky, I'm just left with a lame leg. My brother, he died of it later."

"Life's hard," said Paddy nervously.

"So is death," said the fox. "As you are about to find out. Have you any last words to say before I bite your head off?"

"Indeed I have," said Paddy. And shouting *"Help!"* at the top of his voice, he ran for the nearest cover.

Dada, waiting with his gun at the bottom of the wood, heard nothing, of course, but the cry came loud and clear to Brigid. The voice was unmistakable, and she dashed in among the trees. No thought of possible danger to Paddy from the fox had occurred to her, so that the scene that met her eyes was all the more terrible.

Paddy had had time—because the fox was lame and slow—to scramble up into the top of a bush. But the bush was not tall enough, and his legs were still in range of fox-jump. To her horror Brigid saw the snarling fox leap and apparently bite off one of Paddy's feet.

As if in a dream, Brigid charged at the fox. She had no gun like Dada had, not even a stick to strike with, but she ran furiously, straight at the enemy.

The fox dropped his spoils and fled, three-legged, back through the wood, and the leprechaun tumbled out of the bush to lie sprawled upon the ground.

Kneeling beside him, Brigid forced herself to look at his legs and felt sick with relief when she realized what it was that the fox had torn off. It was not a foot but a frog-skin boot.

She looked to see if Paddy was hurt elsewhere, but it did not seem so.

"Paddy," she said, gently patting his green cheeks, pale now as lime juice, "are you all right?"

PADDY'S POT OF GOLD

Slowly Paddy opened his eyes. Gingerly he levered himself into a sitting position.

"Dear girl, dear girl," he said in a shaky voice, "you saved my life. But for you that would have been the end of Patrick Victorious Wellington Right-Handed O'Reilly. Dead it is I would have been."

Suddenly the pigeons clattered out of the treetops as from the bottom end of the wood there came the crash of a single gunshot.

"As he is," said Brigid.

CHAPTER 9

Under the Elder Tree

Paddy was badly shaken, it was plain. Suddenly
he looked his age, all one hundred and seventy-
four years of it, and his little green hands, Brigid
could see, were trembling.

"It's a good thing you're a cobbler and can
mend this," she said as she put his boot back on
for him, for the fox's teeth had ripped it. But
Paddy only muttered something about "No
need to bother now."

She carried him home, cradling him in her
arms, and put him down by the entrance to his
lodgings.

"Have a good sleep, now," she said.
"You've had an awful shock."

She watched him go none too steadily down
his hole and then walked back through the
wood. Dada was waiting for her, gun in one
hand, the other holding up the dead fox by its
tail.

"He broke right for me," said Dada. "You must have frightened him."

"I did," said Brigid. She shivered.

"Not cold, are you?" said Dada. "The weather's still mild."

"Not for long," Brigid said. "There's a big freeze coming in for the new year."

"Oh, there is, is there!" Dada laughed. "And who told you that? One of the little people, I suppose! Well, it'll have to hurry, this big freeze. There are only a couple of days of this year left."

I do hope I see Paddy before the weather changes, thought Brigid as they walked home. What shall I do, though? I don't like to disturb him, banging on the elder tree—he wasn't at all pleased last time. Perhaps he'll feel well enough to come down to the farm tomorrow.

But there was no sign of him on the next day. On the day after that, the last one of the old year, the skies turned gray, the wind backed into the northeast, and at midday the weathercaster on the radio predicted snow. Dada, listening, shot a glance at his daughter, then smiled and shook his head in puzzlement.

After lunch Brigid went to see Snowy, taking him a crust of stale bread that Mother had given her, and there, walking slowly up the garden path beside the carrot patch where she had first seen him, was Paddy.

He was a better color, Brigid saw, but he did not look like his old jaunty self. He was not smoking either, she noticed. With his usual ability to read her thoughts, he took the nose warmer out of his pocket, looked at it rather wistfully, and put it away again.

"Have you run out of seaweed tobacco?" asked Brigid.

"No, no."

"Are you giving up smoking, then?"

"One of these days."

"Oh," said Brigid, puzzled. "Anyway, I'm glad to see you, Paddy. The badgers were right. There's going to be a lot of snow, the forecast says so, so soon I won't be seeing you, I suppose?"

"You will not," said Paddy.

"I've just been saying my good-byes," he went on. "To Snowy and old Fillpail and old Neddy and the pigs."

"Saying your good-byes? Oh, I see, you mean before you hibernate."

"But that still leaves one very important person to say good-bye to," said Paddy, and his green face crinkled into something like the old grin.

"Me?"

"You. You who are my friend. You who gave me a grand bottle for Christmas. You who saved my life. Give us your finger, dear girl."

Brigid put out one finger, and the leprechaun grasped it and held it tightly.

"Good-bye now, Brigid," he said. "Hasn't it been the great pleasure to know you."

"Goodness me!" said Brigid. "You talk as though we were never going to meet again!"

Paddy made no reply to this. Instead he pulled out his purse and took from it the shilling and held it out to her.

"A present for you," he said.

"But you mustn't, Paddy," said Brigid. "It's all you have in the world."

"It is and it isn't," said Paddy. "But maybe you're right."

He put the coin back into the purse.

"I'll tell you what," he said. "I'll teach you a little rhyme. A bit of a riddle it is. It might come in useful one day."

"All right," said Brigid. He's never going to give much away, she thought.

"Here it is, then," said Paddy.

> "From Jack's door to Eve's fruit.
> Fifty paces of the boot.
> Cut the fifty into two.
> Adam delved and so must you."

"What a funny rhyme," said Brigid. "What does it mean?"

"No need to worry your head about it now," said Paddy. "Just you learn it by heart. Listen again." And he repeated it.

As soon as he was sure that Brigid had learned it correctly, he said, "You have it entirely. Think about it later."

"When?"

"When you hear the first cuckoo. And now take me home, Brigid, if you'll be so kind, for the old woman is plucking her goose." And Brigid looked up to see the first fat snowflakes wafting slowly down out of the sky.

They reached the tump and climbed its sides, already whitening, and Brigid set Paddy down before his hole. She squatted in front of him and fondly ruffled the red hair and looked into the green eyes and said, "Down you go now, and have a good long sleep."

"I will, dear girl," said P.V.W.R.H. O'Reilly. "Indeed I will." And he turned and disappeared from her sight.

That New Year's Eve the snow fell stead-

ily, and on New Year's Day as well, and the land was covered thick with it.

Brigid made a snowman on the lawn that Dada had been going to cut all in good time. It was a white snowman, of course, it had to be, but she put a red woolly hat on its head and stuck two brussels sprouts in its face to give it green eyes, and she carved from a bit of wood what looked like a short pipe and stuck it into its mouth.

For a month and more the snow lay, and even when February Fillditch at last washed it away the days were still cold and raw, and Brigid was glad that Paddy was six feet underground. But when March went out like a lion and April came in like a lamb and there was still no sign of him, she went anxiously to the badgers' set and banged with her banging stick. Day after day she banged, but he did not appear.

Night after night Brigid lay in bed trying to persuade herself that Paddy was simply sleeping still, and morning after morning she woke feeling more and more sure that he would never wake again.

Then one day, awake very early and listening to the birds' dawn chorus, she heard a snorting, snuffling noise coming from below her window. She jumped out of bed and looked down, and there below, broad striped head raised, was the great boar badger.

At the sight of her he turned and shuffled off toward the wood, stopping every few yards to look back. The message was plain—follow—

and Brigid dressed quickly and slipped quietly out of the house.

She did not see the boar again, but when she reached the tump, she saw what he had come to tell her.

Under the elder tree that she had banged so often there was no longer any sign of Paddy's entrance hole. Where it had been there was now a mound of freshly dug earth, scored with claw marks and studded with paw prints.

The landlords had filled in the lodger's grave.

CHAPTER 10

In the Orchard

I must be sensible about it, Brigid told herself. To die in your sleep without pain or suffering, after such a long, long happy life—why, surely no one could ask for more. But I will miss him! Never to see that funny old wrinkled green face again, with its mop of red hair, never to smell the smoke curling from his nose warmer, never to hear that cackling laugh—all I've got left are memories. Ah, but wait—he left me that rhyme, didn't he?

And even as the thought went through her head she heard the call of the first cuckoo.

"Now," said Brigid, "can I remember it? Let's see . . .

"From Jack's door to Eve's fruit.
Fifty paces of the boot.
Cut the fifty into two.
Adam delved and so must you.

"But what in the world does it mean?"

Back in her room she found paper and a pen and wrote down the four lines and looked at them. Adam and Eve are in it, she thought, so does it have to do with a garden? Our garden? That's where I first met Paddy, after all. But who's Jack? I don't know anyone named Jack. And what does "delved" mean? The only easy part is the fifty paces. "Cut the fifty into two," so it's twenty-five paces from somewhere to somewhere.

At breakfast she said, "D'you know anyone named Jack?"

"No," said Mother. "Why?"

"Oh, it's just a riddle someone told me. I can't make sense of it. We haven't got an animal named Jack, have we? A pig or something?"

"No," said Dada, "but we do have an animal that *is* a jack. Neddy. He-donkeys are called jacks."

"Jack's door" must be the door of Neddy's old shed in the orchard, then!

"What's Eve's fruit?" Brigid asked.

"Eve's fruit?" said Mother. "Why, the apple, I suppose. Eve was tempted in the Garden of Eden and ate the apple. Anything else you want to know for your funny old riddle?"

"Just one thing," Brigid said. She was trying hard to keep the excitement out of her voice. Neddy's door and one of the apple trees—one that was fifty paces away! There was something halfway between them!

Adam delved and so must you. "What does 'delved' mean?" she asked.

"It means 'dug,' " said Dada. "To delve is to dig."

"Thanks," said Brigid.

She made herself finish her breakfast, chewing especially slowly while her mind raced. "It might come in useful one day." She remembered Paddy's exact words when he told her the rhyme. Could it be . . . ! Could it?

Out in the orchard she stood spade in hand by Neddy's door and looked at the apple trees, six in all. Four of them were much too far away—she could see that without pacing it out—and one was much too close, hardly more than a dozen feet away. But the sixth one looked about right. Counting out loud, she stepped the distance to it. Fifty paces exactly!

She turned and came back toward the donkey's shed, counting again. *Fifty paces of the boot. Cut the fifty into two.*

And at twenty-five she stopped. Now at last she allowed herself to believe!

Every leprechaun has a pot of gold buried somewhere. Here it was, under her feet! Brigid began to dig.

Dada's big spade was awkward for her to handle, but luckily the ground was soft, and before long she had made quite a big hole. Every moment she expected the spade to strike something, but there was nothing but earth and more earth.

Brigid sat down on the edge of the hole to rest and took the piece of paper from her pocket. Had she gotten something wrong? "Fifty paces of the boot," she read again, and then suddenly she jumped up! Of course, they were *his* paces, not hers! Each step of hers must be a foot long, each step of his more like three inches. It was between "Jack's door" and the *nearest* apple tree!

Once she had measured the halfway point and begun to dig, it was only a matter of minutes before the edge of the spade struck something hard.

Afterward—for ages afterward—neither Mother nor Dada could really believe what had happened.

Hardly a day passed when Dada, milking his new cows, tending his new sheep, or driving his new tractor, did not recall with amazement how Brigid had shouted, how he had come running, how between them they had dug out a heavy squat oak chest bound with brass bands.

Hardly a day passed when Mother, drawing her new curtains, cleaning her new carpets, or loading her new washing machine, did not remember with wonder how she had come rushing to see what all the fuss was about, and how Dada had broken the padlock ("Paddylock," Brigid said to herself) with a blow of the spade edge and opened the lid.

The little chest was filled to the brim with coins—gold coins—gold sovereigns! Old coins

they were, too, bearing the head of King George III.

"That makes them even more valuable," said Dada, picking one out at random. "Why, look, this one is dated 1815."

"Oh!" cried Brigid. "Why, that was when—" And she stopped suddenly.

"When what?"

"When the Battle of Waterloo was fought."

"Clever girl! And the cleverest girl there ever was to find this buried treasure! Why, we won't ever need to worry about money again!"

Afterward, out of Brigid's hearing, Mother and Dada had agreed that they would not question her, would never question her, about how she had come upon the treasure chest.

"Strange though," one said. "D'you remember on her birthday we were talking about leprechauns?"

"And how each had a pot of gold buried somewhere?"

"Maybe Brigid had her own private leprechaun."

They looked at each other and laughed rather self-consciously.

As for Brigid, she was, naturally, very excited. She was not a greedy person, but it was nice to think that she could afford things like a new bike and that she could put a lot into a savings account.

"They're mean, leprechauns are. Stingy," Dada had said. But not this one. Now that shilling really was all he had in the world.

Later, when all the fuss had died down, Brigid went to the tump. It was a beautiful spring day, and the wood was bursting with new life.

In the Orchard

In her pocket she had a pruning knife of
Dada's and a felt-tipped marker of Mother's.
She climbed the tump and stood by the elder
tree but not to bang this time, for there was no
one to hear but the badgers.

With the knife she sliced away a square sec-
tion of the rough bark to show the white wood
underneath, and on this she wrote with the
marker in large, careful black capital letters:

P.V.W.R.H. O'REILLY
1815–1990

As she stood for a moment looking at her
handiwork, she heard somewhere in the depths
of the wood a familiar cackling laugh.

It was only the cry of the green woodpecker,
of course.

Well, it must have been.

Mustn't it?

DICK KING-SMITH was born and raised in Gloucestershire, England. He served in the Grenadier Guards in World War II, then returned home to Gloucestershire to realize his lifelong ambition of farming. After twenty years as a farmer, he turned to teaching and then to writing the children's books that have earned him many fans on both sides of the Atlantic. Inspiration for his writing comes from his farm and his animals.

Among his well-loved novels are *Babe: The Gallant Pig, Harry's Mad, Martin's Mice* (all American Library Association Notable Books); *Ace: The Very Important Pig* (a *School Library Journal* Best Book of the Year); and *The Toby Man* (a Junior Library Guild selection).